Written by Chantelle Naude
Illustrated by Saad at Pxltd Palette

Once, there lived a brave and curious girl named Scarlett.
Scarlett loved playing with her friend, exploring the outdoors and eating lots of yummy treats.

One quiet night at home, Scarlett started feeling very tired and thirsty for many, many days. She couldn't seem to quench her thirst no matter how much water she drank. Mum and Dad were very worried and took her to the hospital. After some tests with lots of friendly doctors and nurses, Scarlett was diagnosed with a condition called type 1 diabetes.

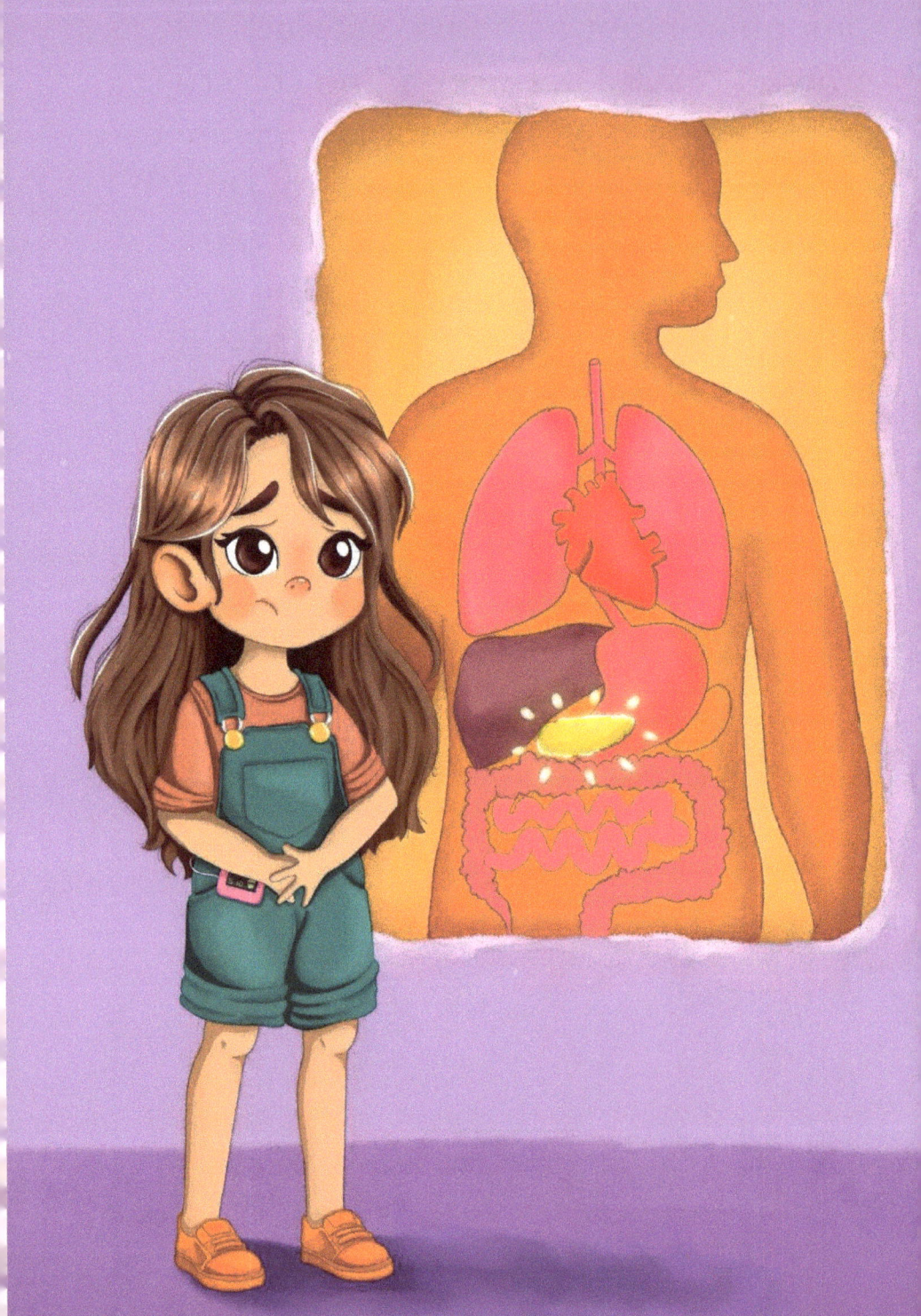

Type 1 diabetes is a condition where your body doesn't make enough insulin. Insulin is made in an organ called the pancreas. It's a hormone that helps our bodies use the sugar we get from food for energy. Without enough insulin, the sugar stays in your blood, causing high blood sugar levels, and this will make you very sick.

Scarlett and her parents learned that managing her diabetes meant she had to take good care of herself. She needed to keep active and eat healthy foods like fruits, vegetables, and whole grains.
She also had to take insulin injections or use an insulin pump, which gave her the right amount of insulin to help her body use the sugar properly.

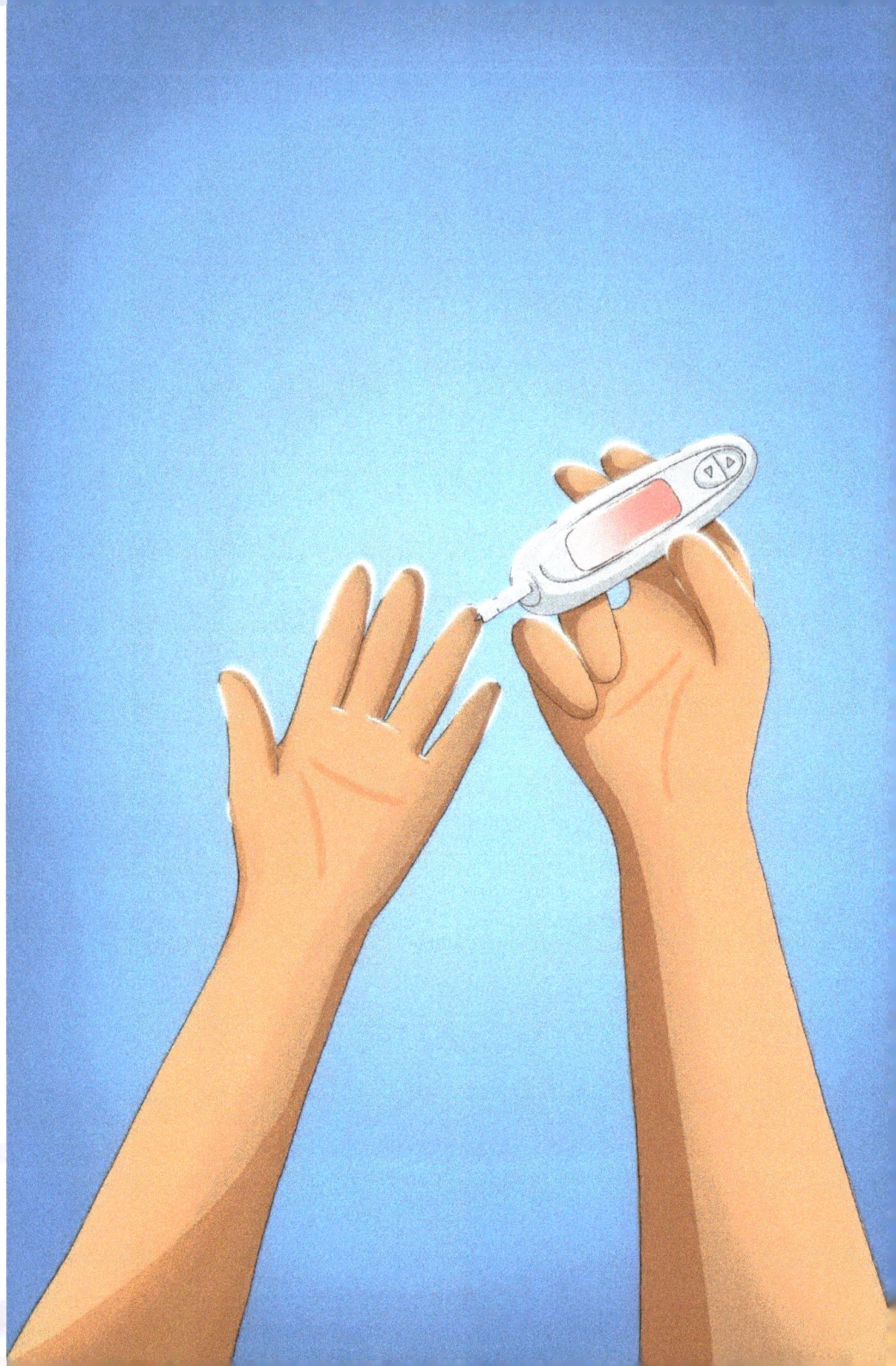

Scarlett learned that she needed to monitor her blood sugar levels regularly. Mum, Dad, and Scarlett learned how to use a special device called a glucometer, which checked her blood sugar through finger pricks.

It helped to tell if her blood sugar was too high or too low, so she could take the right steps and stay healthy.

Scarlett's journey with type 1 diabetes taught Mum, Dad, and Scarlett about counting carbohydrates. Carbohydrates are found in foods like bread, pasta, and cookies. She learned that she needed to keep track of how many carbohydrates she ate so that she could adjust her insulin dose to what she needed.

She used a Continuous Glucose Monitor (CGM) to help her electronically measure her glucose levels so that she didn't have to do so many finger pricks throughout the day.

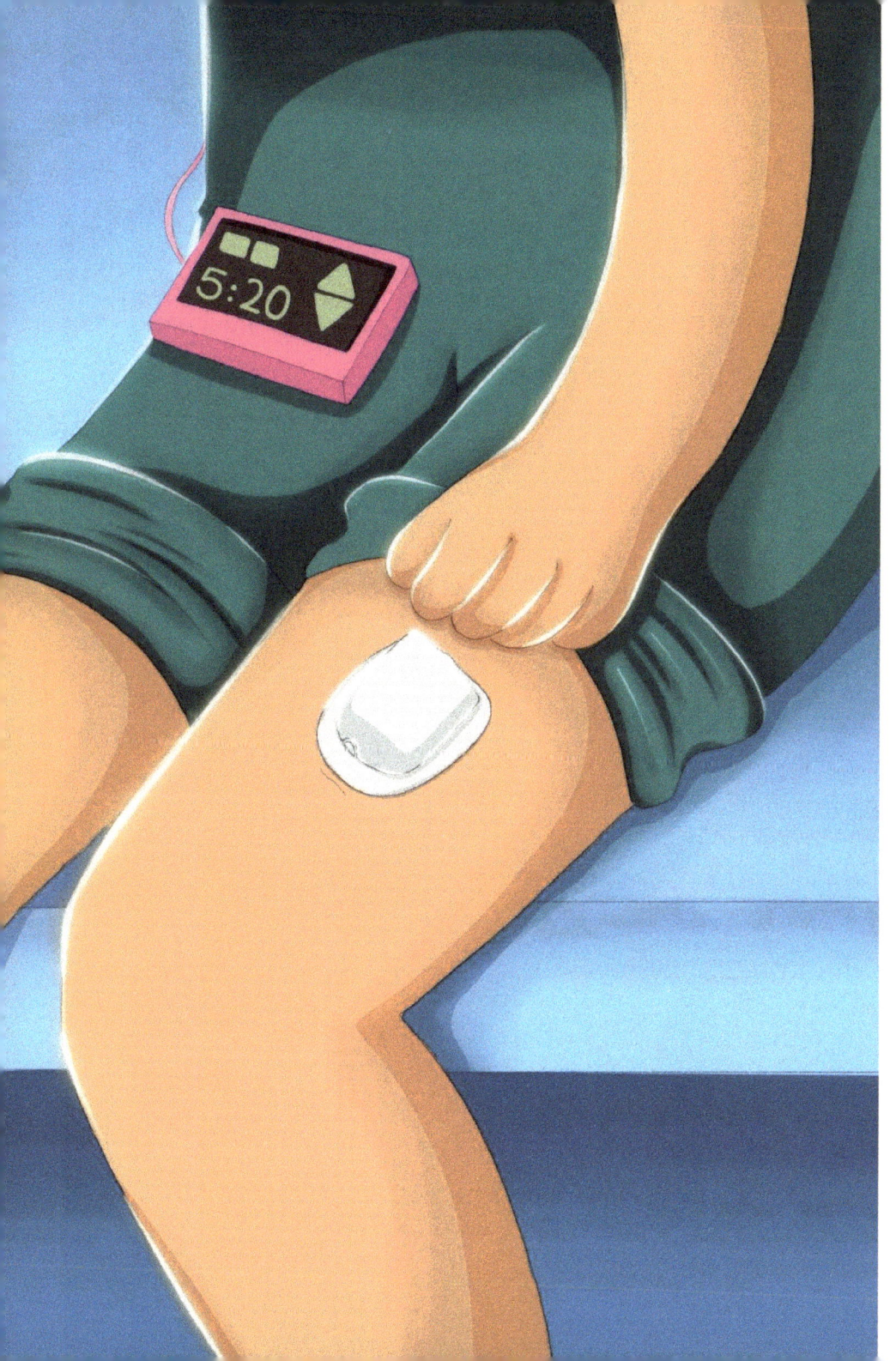

Scarlett loved playing games and being active. She found out that exercise was not only fun but also helped her manage her diabetes.

When she was having fun and being active, her body used up the sugar in her blood, which helped keep her blood sugar levels in a healthy range.

Sometimes, Scarlett's blood sugar would drop too low, which made her feel very shaky, sweaty, and weak.
She learned that in those situations, all she needed to do was to sit down and eat or drink something sugary, like glucose tablets or juice, wait 15 minutes, and then eat a piece of fruit or have some milk once her sugar levels were back in range.

Scarlett learned that even on special occasions, like birthdays or holidays, she could still enjoy lots of yummy treats. She learned how to balance her food choices, count carbohydrates, and take her insulin to keep her blood sugar in balance so she could always still have a piece of cake or a big cookie!

Scarlett's friends and family learned all about her type 1 diabetes and wanted to support her too. They learned how to recognise the signs of low blood sugar so they could help Scarlett when she needed it.

They were always there to play and have fun, making Scarlett feel loved and included.

Scarlett learned that the healthy habits she developed by managing her diabetes were beneficial for everyone, not just for people with diabetes. Eating healthy foods, staying active, and taking care of our bodies are important for everyone's well-being.

What does a typical day with type 1 diabetes looked like for Scarlett?
She woke up, checked her blood sugar, took her insulin, ate a healthy breakfast, and went to school. She had fun with her friends, she managed her blood sugar levels, and enjoyed her life just like everyone else.

Throughout Scarlett's adventure, her family and medical team were always by her side. Mum and Dad encouraged her to be strong and learned to take care of her diabetes with their support. The doctors and nurses continue to teach Scarlett and her family everything she needs to know about managing her diabetes, and do their best to answer all of their questions.

As Scarlett grew older, she realized that many people don't understand type 1 diabetes. She decided to become an advocate, which is someone who helps teach people by sharing her story and educating as many people as she can about the condition, because Scarlett wants to help make the world a better and also a less scary place for people with diabetes.

As this part of Scarlett's story comes to an end, she looks forward to many more adventures in her life.
Type 1 diabetes may have brought challenges, but Scarlett knows that with love, support, and knowledge, she can conquer anything that comes her way.

I hope Scarlett's story helped you understand type 1 diabetes a little better.

Remember, everyone's journey is unique and a little bit different, but with the right tools, support, and education, anyone with type 1 diabetes can lead a happy, full, and fulfilling life.

Thank you for joining us and thank you for being so brave!

Charity Organisations

AUS: www.Diabetesaustralia.com.au

USA: www.diabetes.org

EU: www.easd.org

International: www.idf.org

Visit **NotSoScaryBooks.com** for more amazing stories that help us all learn!

 **NotSoScaryBooks.com**

GLOSSARY

- <u>Type 1 Diabetes</u>: A condition where the body's pancreas can't produce or doesn't produce enough insulin.
- <u>Insulin</u>: A hormone that helps the body use sugar for energy.
- <u>Glucometer</u>: A device used to test blood sugar levels.
- <u>Carbohydrates</u>: A type of nutrient found in foods like bread, rice, and fruits.
- <u>Blood Sugar</u>: The amount of sugar in the blood.
- <u>Lancet</u>: A small reusable device that looks like a pen. It's used to make a tiny prick on your finger so you can take a blood test.

An extra Special thanks to:

Lisa, Candice, Jaiden and Kahlia, for all your excitement, encouragement, and support throughout this whole journey.

Saad, who's talent, art, and collaboration created the illustrations to the books.

Nurse Kate and nurse Annette, who's expertise and assistance in medical details made the book what it is

All rights reserved. No part of this publication may be reproduced, distributed, or transmitted in any form or by any means, including photocopying, recording, or other electronic or mechanical methods, without the prior written permission of the author, C.Naude, except in the case of brief quotations embodied in critical reviews and certain other noncommercial uses permitted by copyright law.

For permission requests, write to the author at the address below.
info@notsoscarybooks.com

www.ingramcontent.com/pod-product-compliance
Lightning Source LLC
Chambersburg PA
CBHW042321090526
44585CB00024BA/2780